CLUE SCHOOL
The Case of the Missing Cat

by Cathy Hapka

illustrated by Richard Torrey

SCHOLASTIC INC.

New York Toronto London Auckland Sydney
Mexico City New Delhi Hong Kong Buenos Aires

Welcome to Clue School!

Most schools teach reading, writing, and arithmetic. The Clue School teaches all that and much more.

FACULTY AND STAFF

Commander Clue
Principal

Mr. E
Crime Lab

Ms. Leed
Codes and Clues

Dr. Mayhem
Special Investigations

Agatha
Mascot

Penny Sharp
School Secretary

Arnold Bukworm
Librarian

Clara Klea
Custodia

Here students learn how to hunt for clues, dust for fingerprints, and everything else that you need to know to become a detective. Help the Clue School Kids solve their latest case....

STUDENTS

Sandra Spade

Artie Doyle

Suzy Sluthson

Sam Santiago

Wendy Watson

Hardy Drew

Marlo Kim

Homer Sherlock

Where's Mr. E? the Clue School Kids

wondered as they entered

crime class one rainy afternoon.

"He's late!" Artie said.

"We're supposed to have a test today,"

Wendy added.

Hardy looked hopeful.

"Maybe he won't get here in time

to give it to us!"

"Sorry to disappoint you, Hardy,"

Mr. E said as he strode into the room.

"But your test starts right now.

Tell me, have you noticed anything

unusual about the classroom today?"

The students looked around.

"It looks the same to me," Artie said.

"Hmm," Marlo wondered aloud.

"The desks look the same.

The chalkboard looks the same.

So does the bookshelf."

"I know! The windowsill!" Sam pointed out.

"Agatha's missing!"

Agatha, a fat black cat,

was the school mascot.

She always spent the morning napping

under Ms. Leed's desk

and the afternoon snoozing

on Mr. E's windowsill.

But at the moment,

the windowsill was empty.

"Mystery solved!" Hardy said.

"Did we pass the test?"

"Not quite yet," Mr. E said.

"That was just part one.

Part two: find that cat."

With a wink, he hurried

out of the room,

leaving the kids alone.

"Oh, no!" Artie moaned.

"That cat could be anywhere!"

"Not quite," Sandra said logically.

Sandra was always very logical.

"Agatha hates getting wet, remember?

She would never leave the school

on a rainy day."

"Great. So let's search the school!"

Hardy said.

"Wait," Wendy said, as Hardy rushed
toward the classroom door.
"This is supposed to be a test.
We need to do this right,
just like we've learned
in class. We need to find
suspects and question them."

"Good point," Suzy said.

"First we should search for clues

at the scene of the crime.

That's right here!"

She pointed to the windowsill.

The students looked around carefully.

"A-ha!" Sam cried after a moment.

"This looks like a clue."

He pointed to a set of faint but muddy

footprints on the floor near the windowsill.

The prints led straight out the classroom door.

"Let's follow them!" Wendy cried.

The footprints led all the way

to the school library.

"Maybe someone in there kidnapped Agatha,"

Hardy whispered.

"It couldn't be those kids," Suzy said.

"Their feet are too small."

"And it couldn't be Arnold the librarian,

his feet are too big," Wendy added.

"The footprints were made by women's shoes."

"Let's question Arnold anyway,"
Sam suggested.

"Maybe he saw something unusual."

"Agatha's missing, eh?" Arnold said
when he heard the news. "Haven't seen her."

"Have any women been in here this afternoon?"
Wendy asked him.

Arnold scratched his head.

"Only two I can think of," he said.

"Clara, the custodian, came through with her cleaning cart. And Ms. Leed came through carrying a big, empty, box."

"Clara might have stuck Agatha in her cleaning cart," Marlo suggested.

"She hates the way Agatha sheds

on her nice, clean floors."

"Or Ms. Leed could have carried Agatha

through here in her big box," Sandra added.

"Why?" Sam asked. "Ms. Leed loves Agatha."

Hardy shrugged. "I don't know. But we should

split up and question both of them."

Half the kids went to track down Clara.

They spotted her pushing her cleaning cart.

"Look!" Sandra whispered.

"Her shoes are muddy, and she's all wet!"

"That's not all," Hardy whispered back.

"Her clothes are covered in black fur!"

"We've solved the mystery!" Artie cried.

"Let's go tell Mr. E!"

Just then, the kids heard barking.

A moment later, a large black dog

burst into the hall.

By the end of its leash

it was pulling Dr. Mayhem,

one of Clue School's finest teachers.

"Thanks for walking Baskerville
for me just now, Clara,"
Dr. Mayhem said breathlessly.
"I think he worked out
a lot of his extra energy!"
Baskerville jumped up
and slobbered all over Clara.

At that moment, the other half of the class

was still searching for Ms. Leed.

"I wonder where she could be?" Sam said.

They had checked her classroom.

They had checked the teachers' lounge.

There was no sign of her in either place.

"Look!" Marlo cried, pointing through
the glass doors of the front office.
"Isn't that her raincoat in there?"

"Have you seen Ms. Leed?"

Wendy asked the school secretary, Penny.

Penny shook her head.

"I just got here myself."

Marlo was examining the coat.

"Look!" she cried. "This coat

is covered with black fur!"

"That's Ms. Leed's coat,"

Penny commented.

"So she must be around here somewhere.

She wouldn't dare leave

the building without it—

it's raining cats and dogs out there!"

"Right," Sam added, pointing at the floor.

"She especially wouldn't leave

without her shoes!"

Meanwhile, the first group was
questioning Clara. At least,
they were trying to question her.
Baskerville kept barking and licking their faces.
"Sorry, kids. I won't be bringing Baskerville
back here," Dr. Mayhem assured them.
"Not after the way he chased poor Agatha!"
Hardy gasped. "Did you say Agatha?"

Clara scowled. "That cat," she muttered. "Even her name makes me want to sneeze!"

"Did Baskerville chase her into a hiding place somewhere?" Sandra asked.

"I'm afraid not." Dr. Mayhem shook his head sadly. "He chased her right across the kitchen stove and back to Mr. E's classroom. Burned her paw a bit on the stove, poor thing . . ."

The second group walked down the hall.

"Do you hear barking?" Marlo asked.

"Never mind that," Sam said excitedly.

"There's Ms. Leed!"

The teacher was coming out of

the nurse's office. Both her arms were

dotted with bandages,

and the kids could see

scratches on her face.

"Hello, kids," she said cheerfully.

Wendy frowned.

Those looked a lot like cat scratches.

But there was still no sign of Agatha.

And why would Ms. Leed

want to kidnap Agatha anyway?

A few minutes later, the whole class

was back in Mr. E's classroom.

"Did you pass the test?" the teacher asked.

"We think so," Hardy answered for all of them.

"It was a tricky one. We knew Agatha
wouldn't leave the school by herself
on a rainy day. That meant someone
must have taken her somewhere."
Wendy nodded. "Our best clue
was a set of muddy footprints.
But we couldn't figure out why
anyone would want to take Agatha—"

"—until we figured out

that there's one place a cat hates going,

even more than it hates going

out in the rain," Sam finished.

"And we're planning to visit her there

right after school!"

The Clue School Kids

have solved another mystery!

Can YOU track down

the missing cat?

Solution: The cat was at the vet!

ISBN-13: 978-0-439-89886-7
ISBN-10: 0-439-89886-2

12 11 10 9 8 7 6 5 4 3   7 8 9 10 11/0

Printed in the U.S.A.   23

First Scholastic printing, September 2006

Art direction and design by Cheshire Studio